SEP -- 2016			
NOV 2 8 2016			
DEC 0 7 2016			
APR 0 7 2017			
JUL 1 1 2017			
JAN 1 0 2018			
			PRINTED IN U.S.A.

The big wet balloon

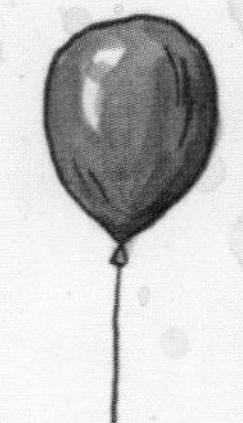

Liniers

THE
BIG WET
BALLOON

A TOON BOOK BY
LINIERS

Spotlight

For Matilda and Clementina...my little muses

Editorial Director: **FRANÇOISE MOULY** · Book Design: **FRANÇOISE MOULY & RICARDO LINIERS SIRI**

RICARDO LINIERS' artwork was done using ink, watercolor, and drops of rain.

ABDOPUBLISHING.COM

Reinforced library bound edition published in 2016 by Spotlight, a division of ABDO
PO Box 398166, Minneapolis, Minnesota 55439. Spotlight produces high-quality reinforced library bound
editions for schools and libraries. Published by agreement with TOON Books.

Printed in the United States of America, North Mankato, Minnesota.
092015
012016

THIS BOOK CONTAINS
RECYCLED MATERIALS

A
TOON
BOOK

www.**TOON-BOOKS**.com

LIBRARY OF CONGRESS CATALOGING-IN-PUBLICATION DATA

This book was previously cataloged with the following information:

Liniers, 1973-
 The big wet balloon : a TOON book / by Liniers.
  pages cm. -- (Easy-to-read comics. Level 2)
Summary: "Matilda promises her little sister Clemmie an amazing weekend spent playing outside. But the
weather's rainy and Clemmie can't bring her new balloon along. Matilda teaches Clemmie all the delights of a
wet Saturday"-- Provided by publisher.
ISBN 978-1-935179-32-0 (alk. paper)
1. Graphic novels. [1. Graphic novels. 2. Sisters--Fiction. 3. Rain and rainfall--Fiction. 4. Balloons--Fiction.] I.
Title.
PZ7.7.L56Bi 2013
741.5'973--dc23
                    2012047662

ISBN 978-1-61479-425-7 (reinforced library bound edition)

Spotlight

A Division of ABDO
abdopublishing.com

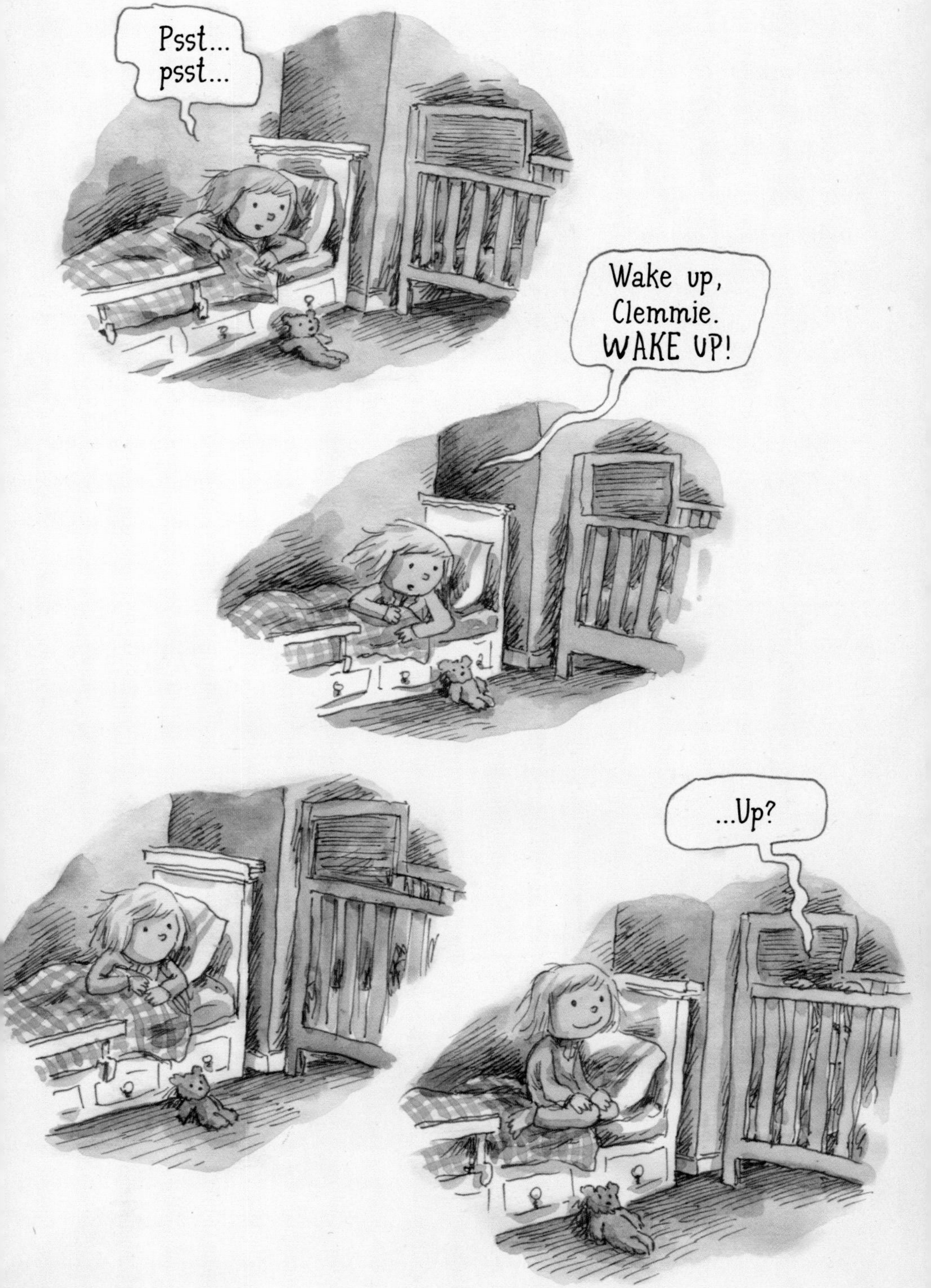
Psst... psst...
Wake up, Clemmie. WAKE UP!
...Up?

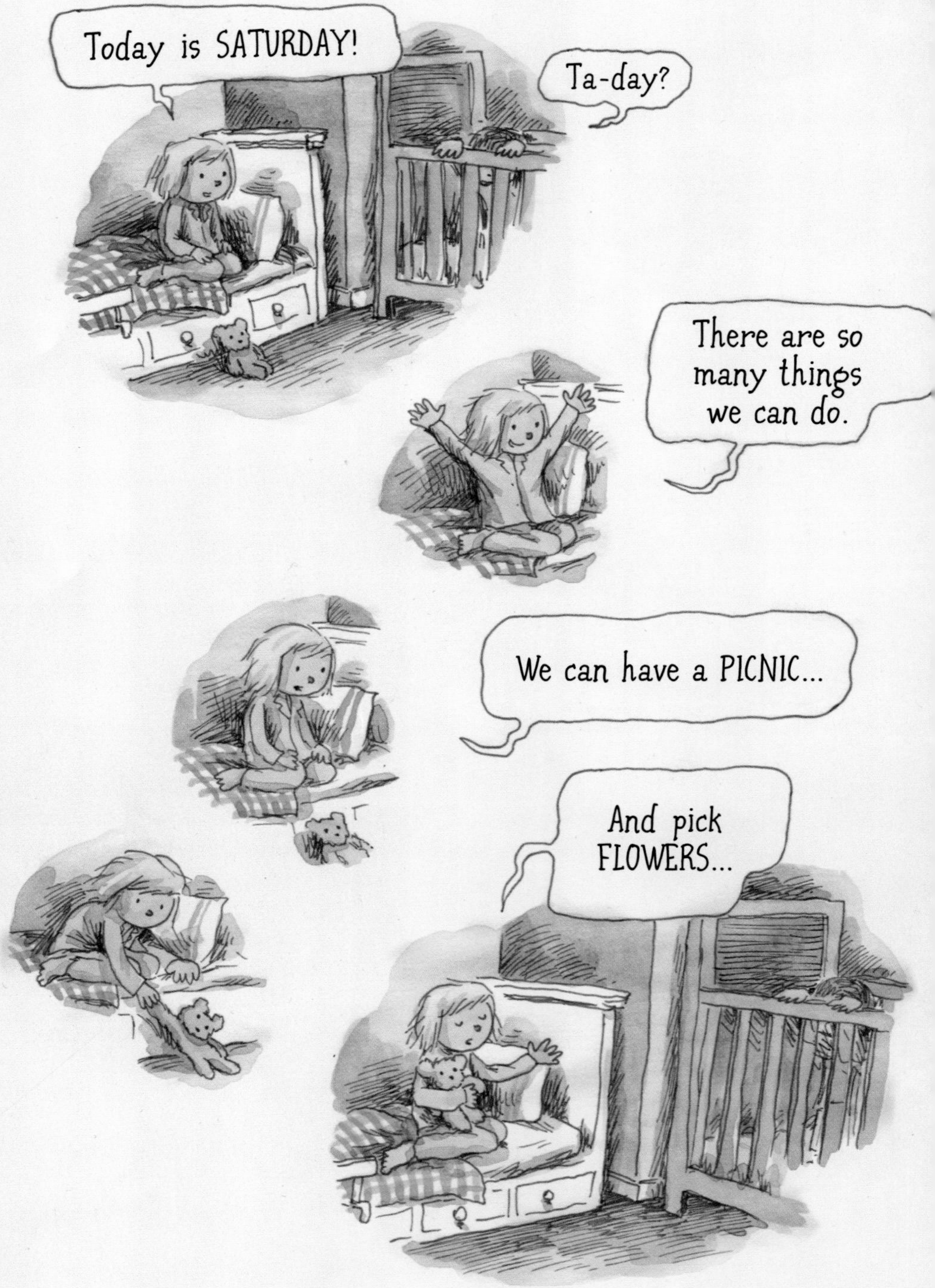
Today is SATURDAY!
Ta-day?
There are so many things we can do.
We can have a PICNIC...
And pick FLOWERS...

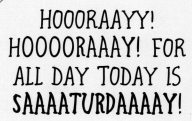

This is how you wake up on Saturday...

HOOORAAYY! HOOOORAAAY! FOR ALL DAY TODAY IS **SAAAATURDAAAAY!**

TA-DAY!

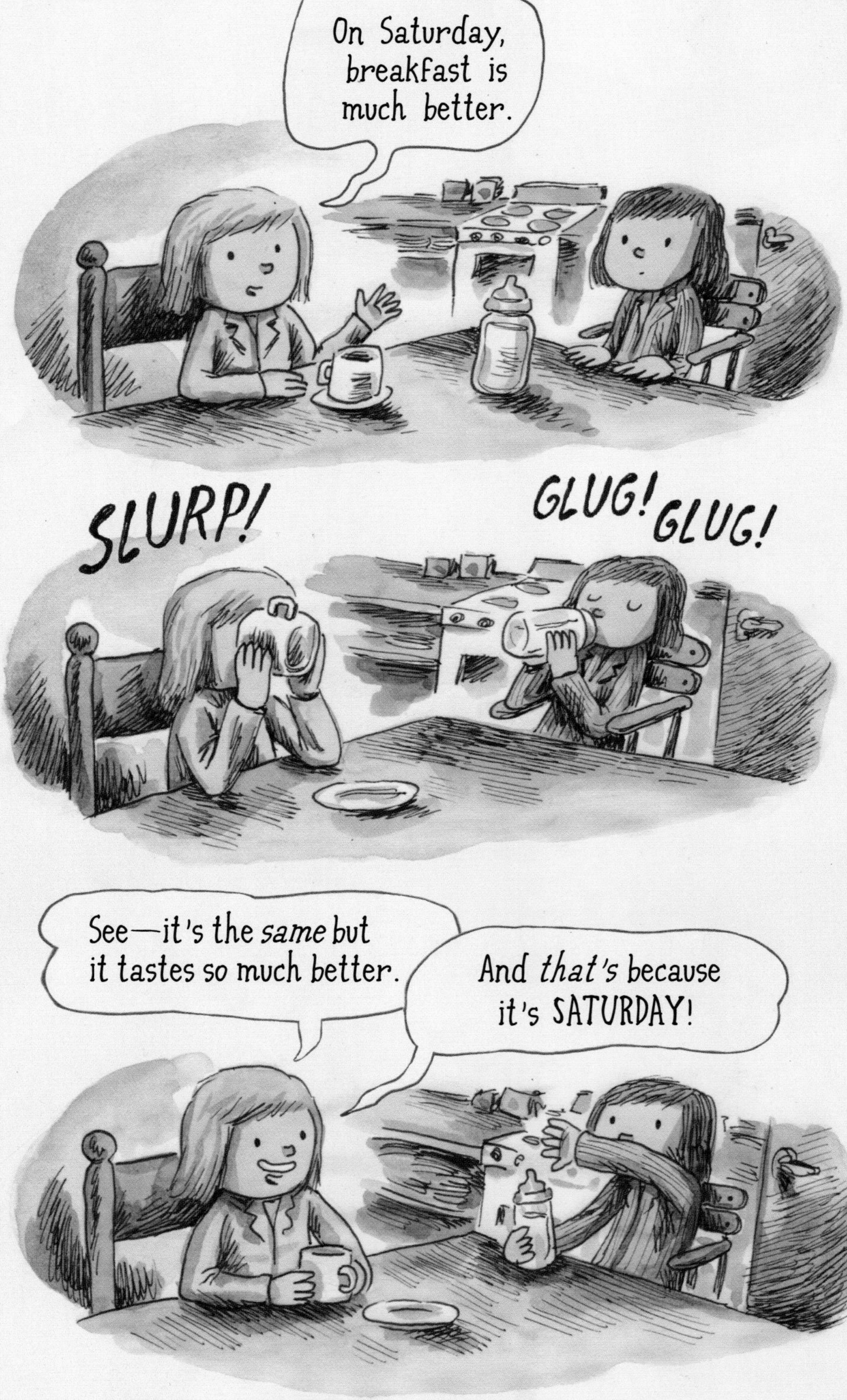
On Saturday, breakfast is much better.
SLURP!
GLUG! GLUG!
See—it's the *same* but it tastes so much better.
And *that's* because it's SATURDAY!

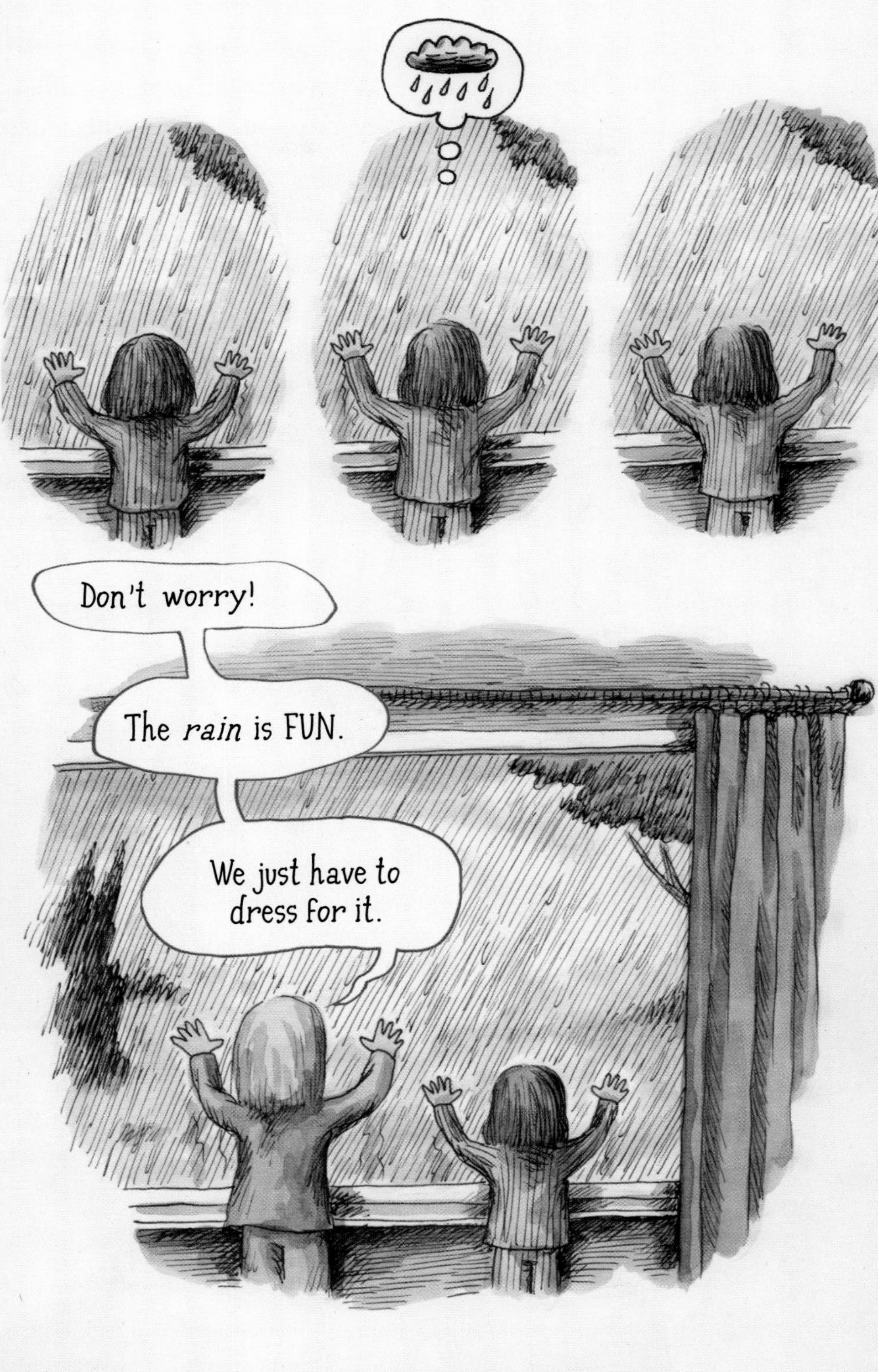
Don't worry!
The *rain* is FUN.
We just have to dress for it.

We have to wear BOOTS! Can you go get your boots?

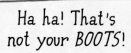

Ha ha! That's not your BOOTS!

That's the red BALLOON from your birthday!

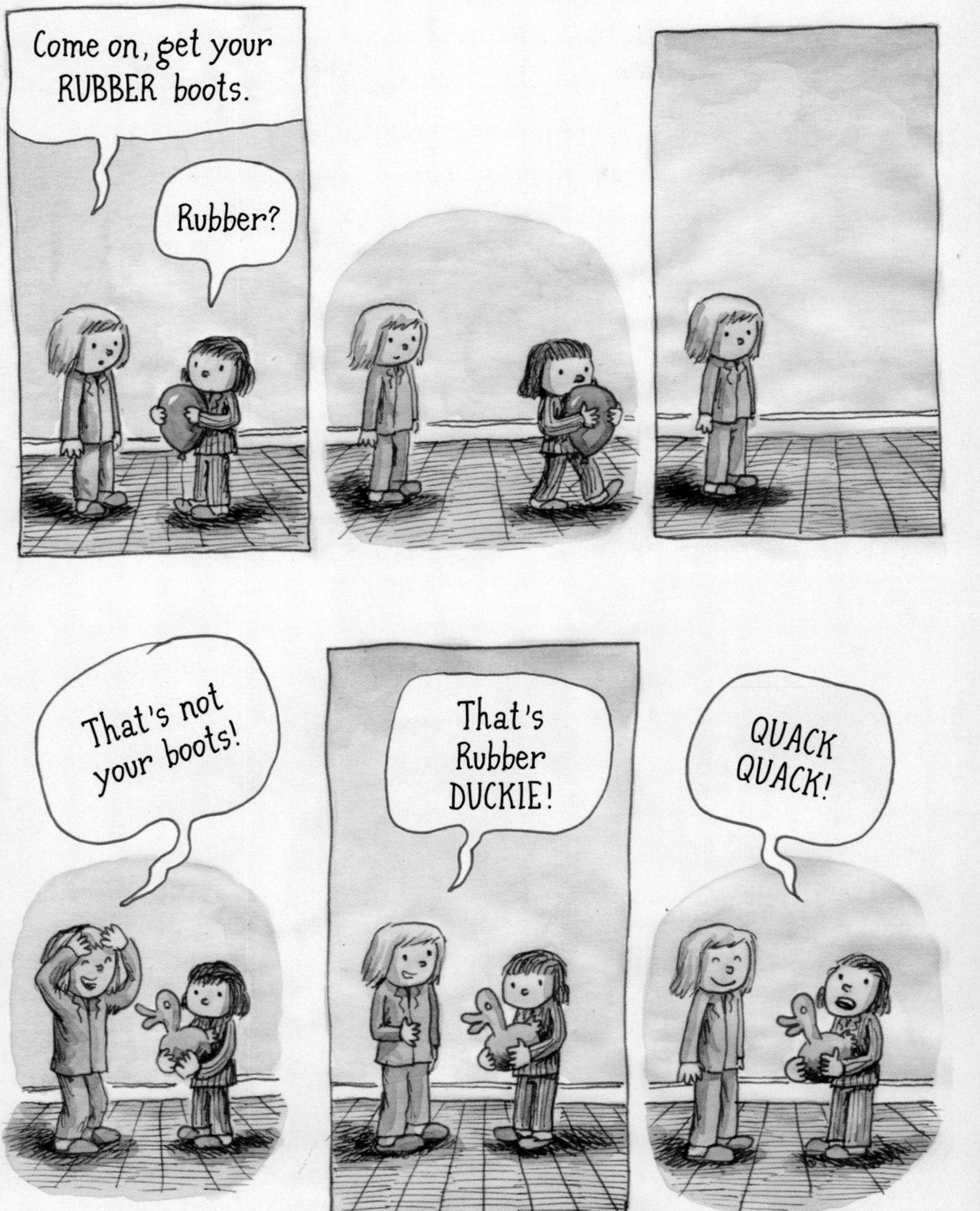
Come on, get your RUBBER boots.
Rubber?
That's not your boots!
That's Rubber DUCKIE!
QUACK QUACK!

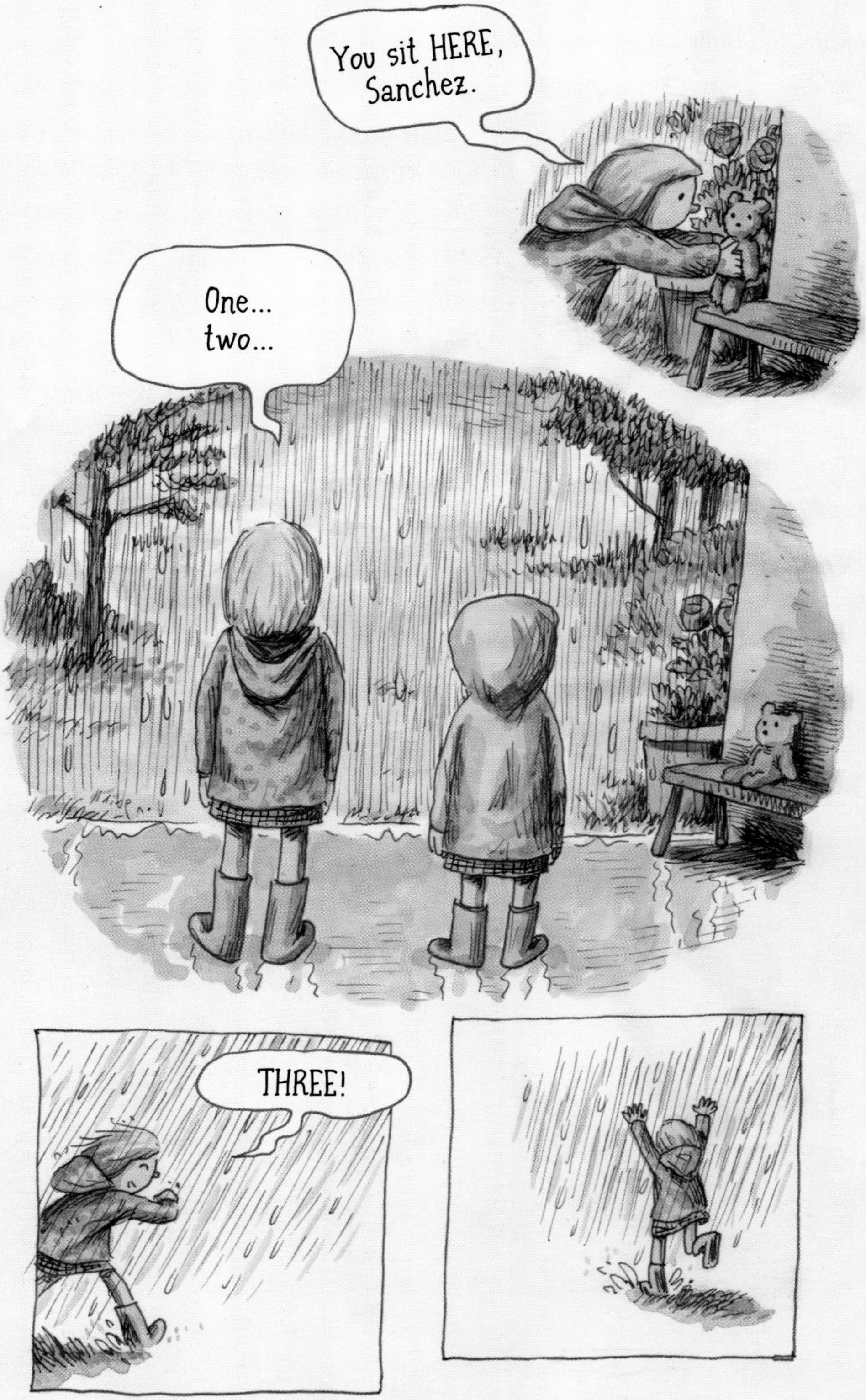
You sit HERE, Sanchez.
One... two...
THREE!

CLEMMIE! You're missing out on all the fun.

Wet!

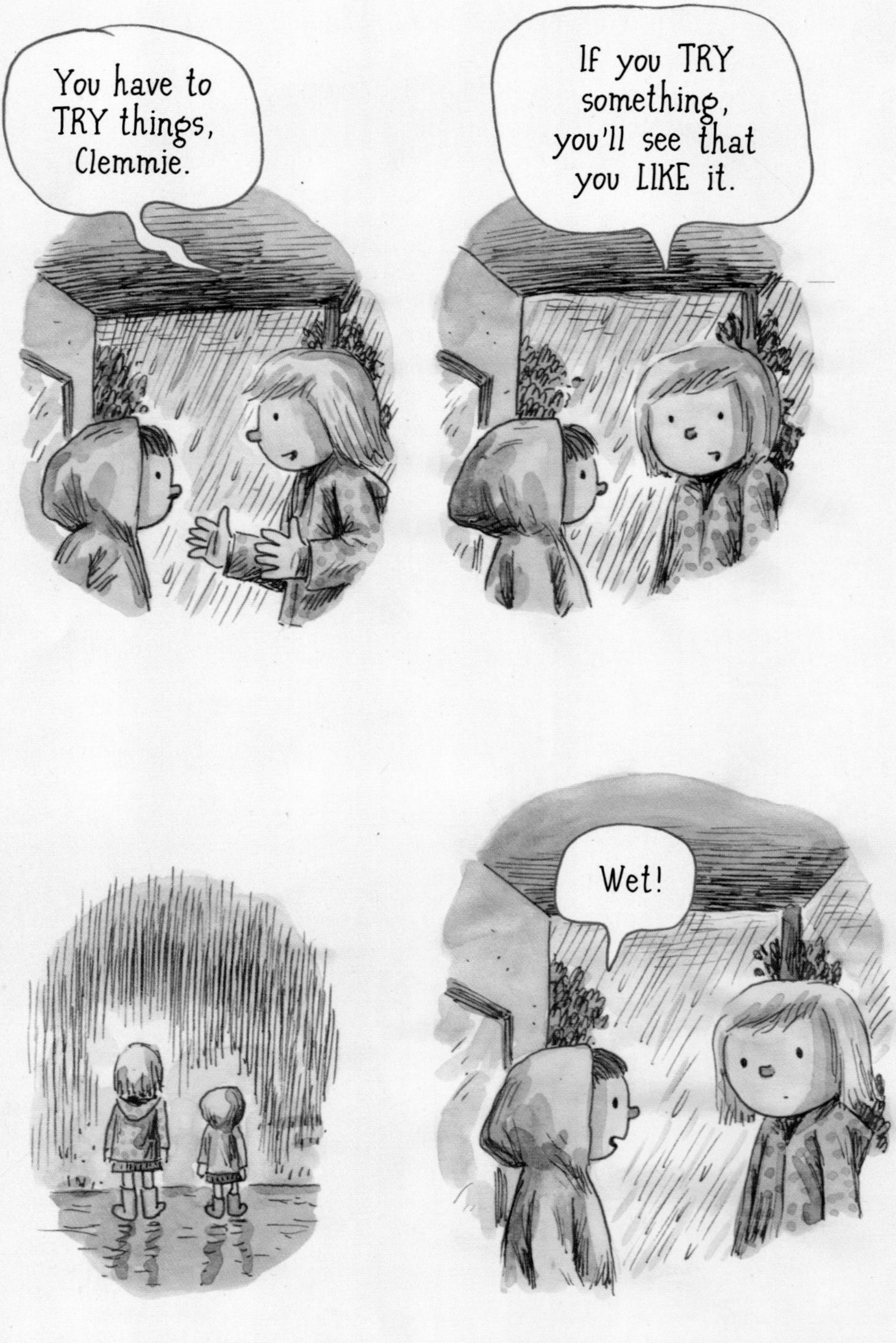
You have to TRY things, Clemmie.
If you TRY something, you'll see that you LIKE it.
Wet!

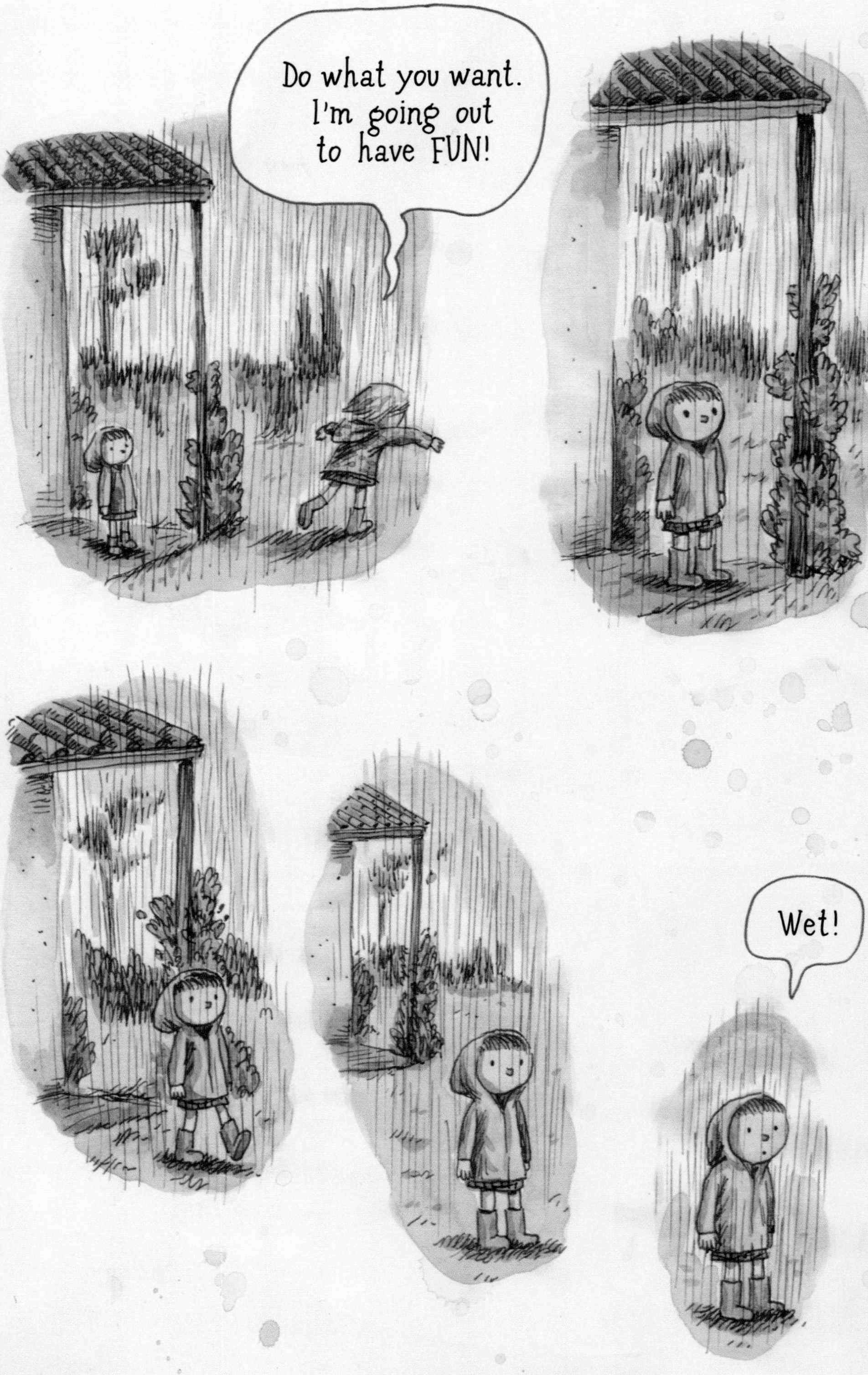
Do what you want. I'm going out to have FUN!
Wet!

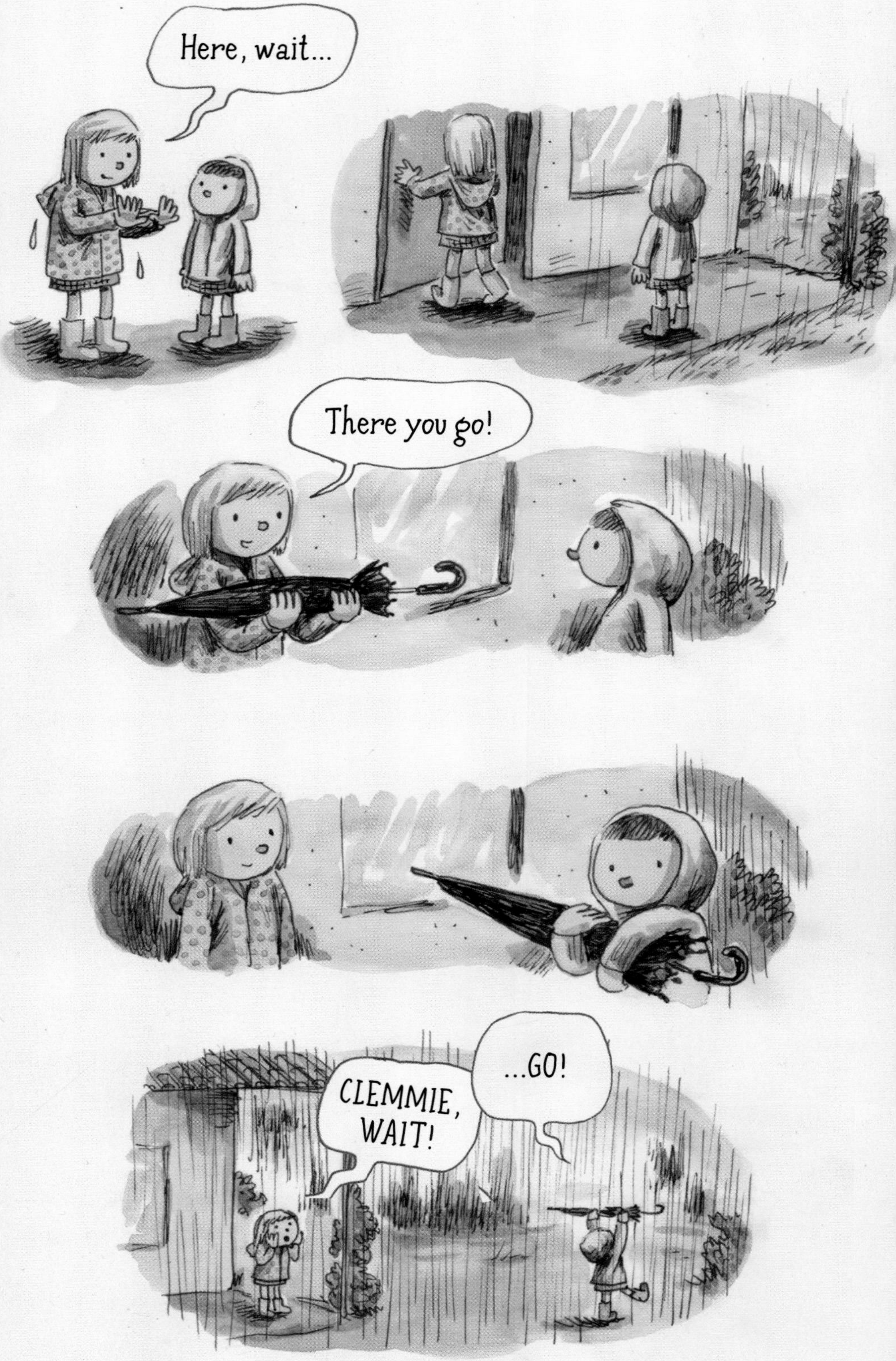
Here, wait...
There you go!
CLEMMIE, WAIT!
...GO!

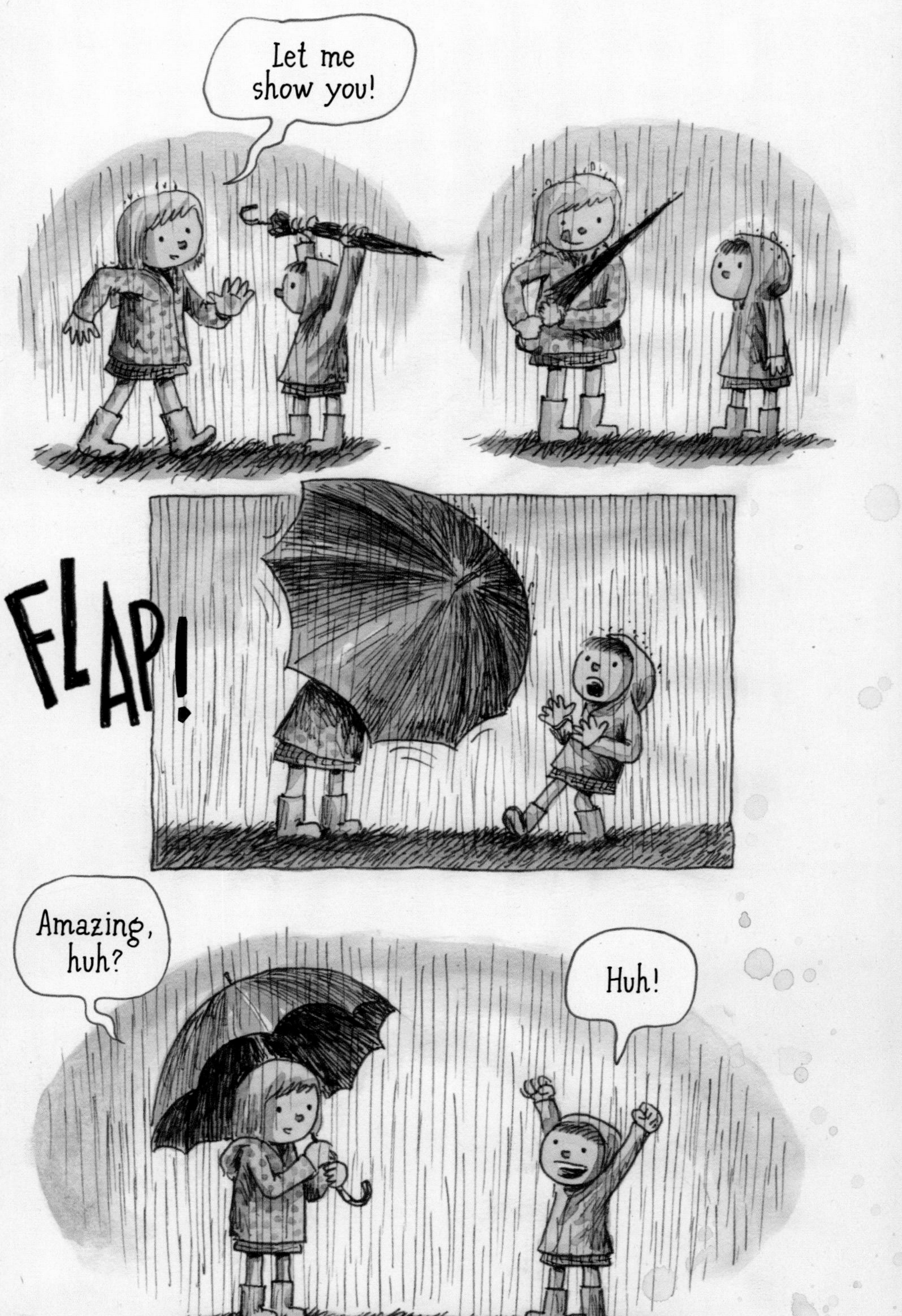
Let me show you!
FLAP!
Amazing, huh?
Huh!

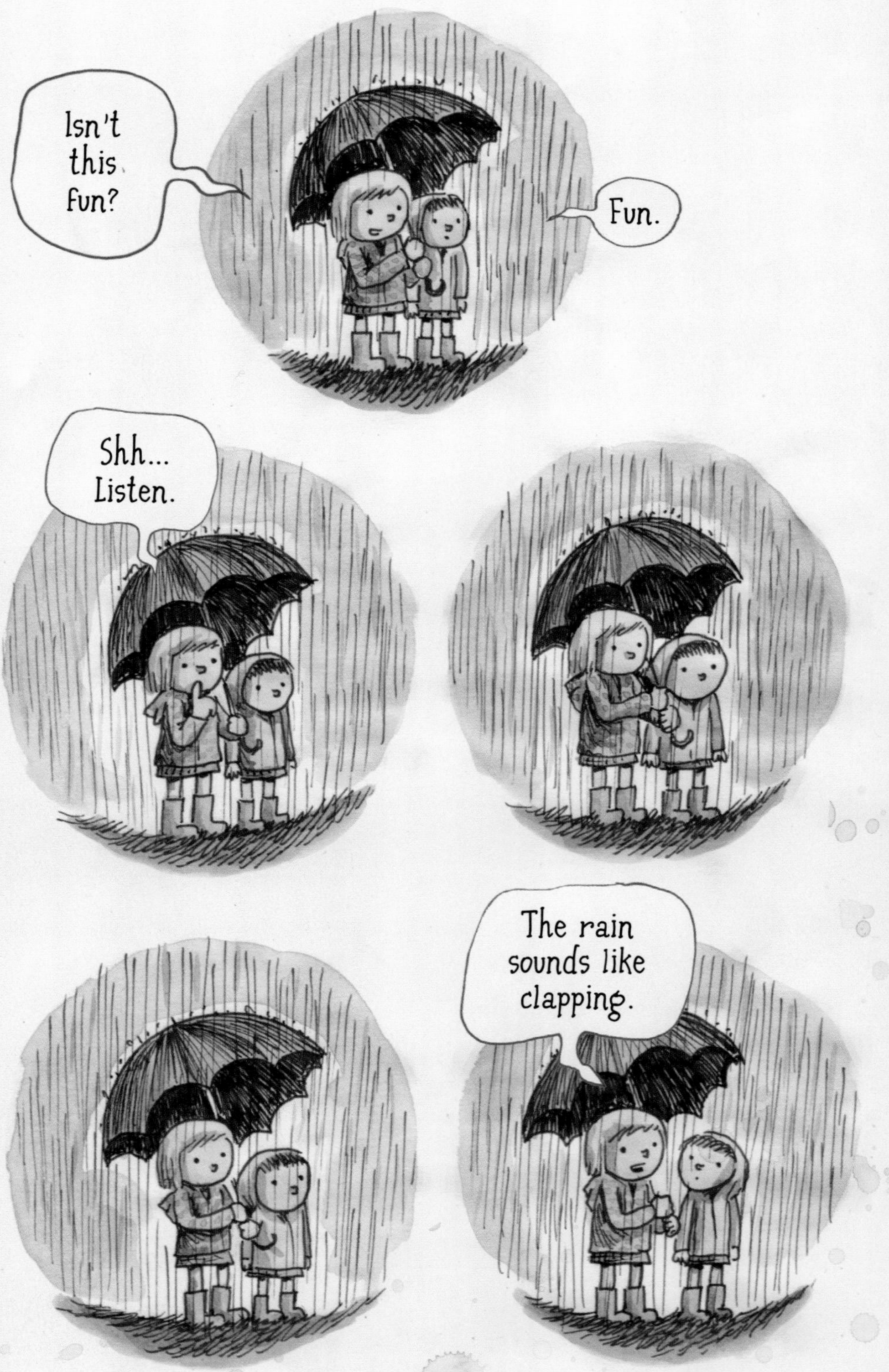
Isn't this fun?
Fun.
Shh... Listen.
The rain sounds like clapping.

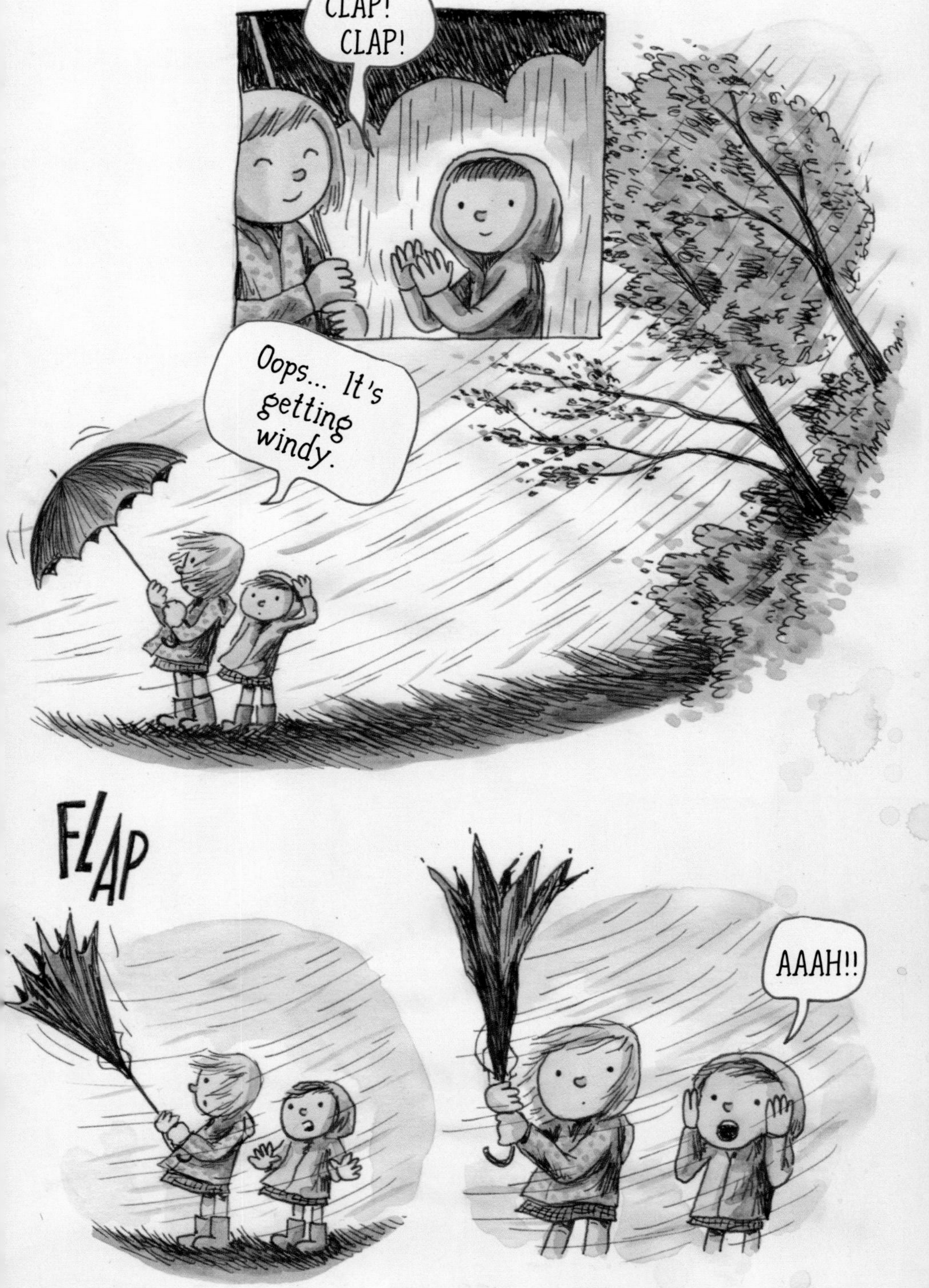
CLAP! CLAP!
Oops... It's getting windy.
FLAP
AAAH!!

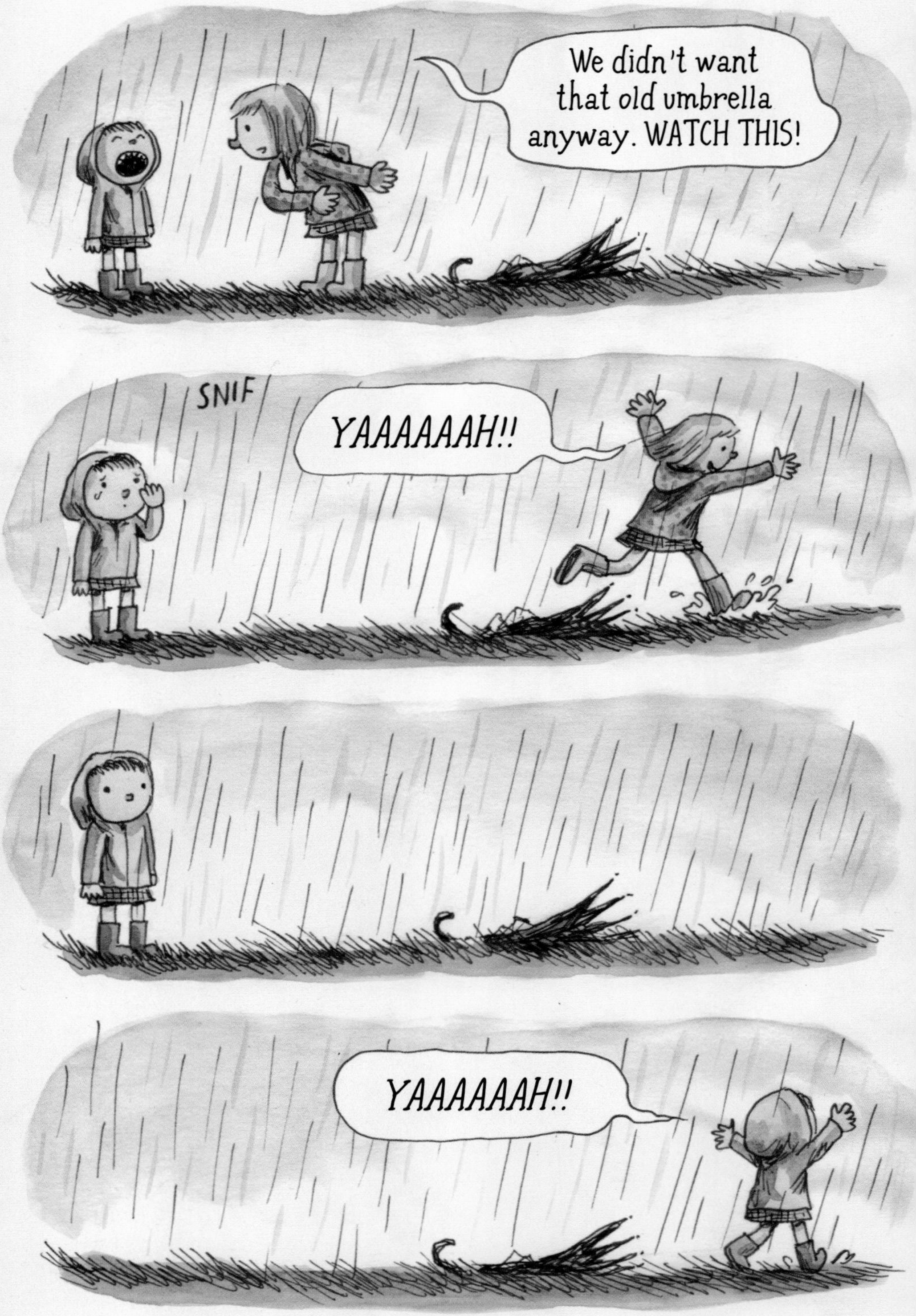
We didn't want that old umbrella anyway. WATCH THIS!
SNIF
YAAAAAAH!!
YAAAAAAH!!

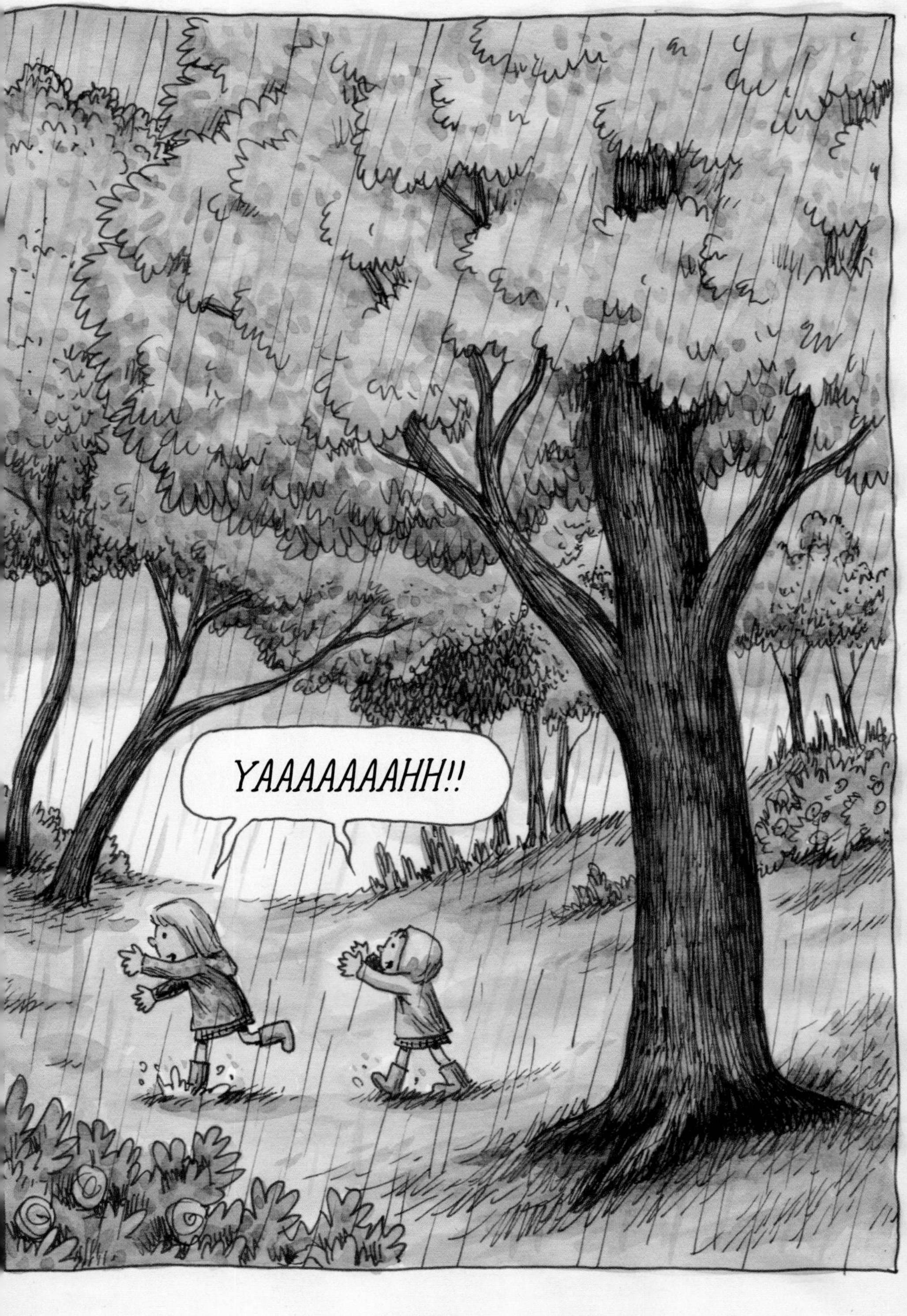
YAAAAAAAHH!!

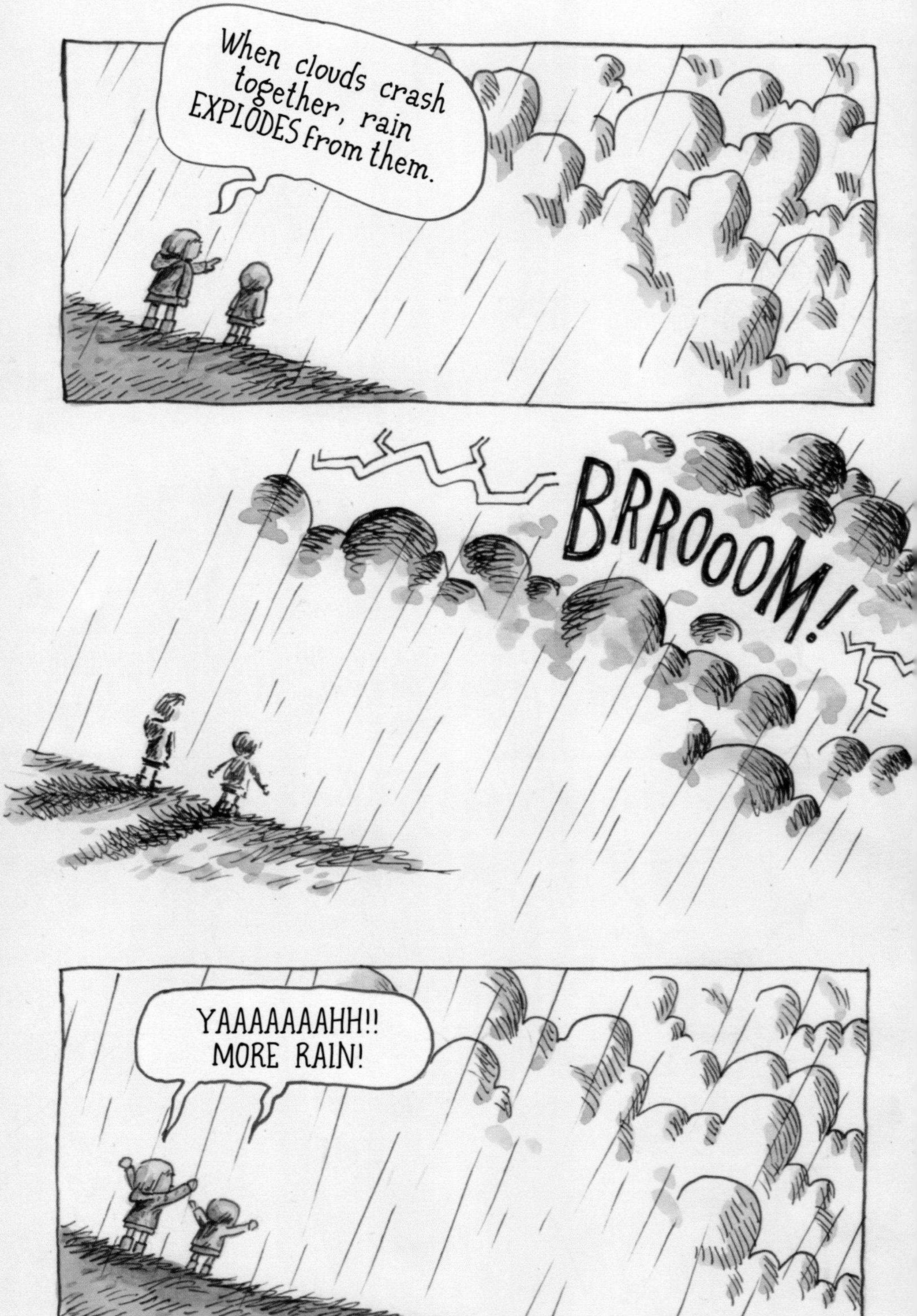
When clouds crash together, rain EXPLODES from them.
BRROOOM!
YAAAAAAAHH!! MORE RAIN!

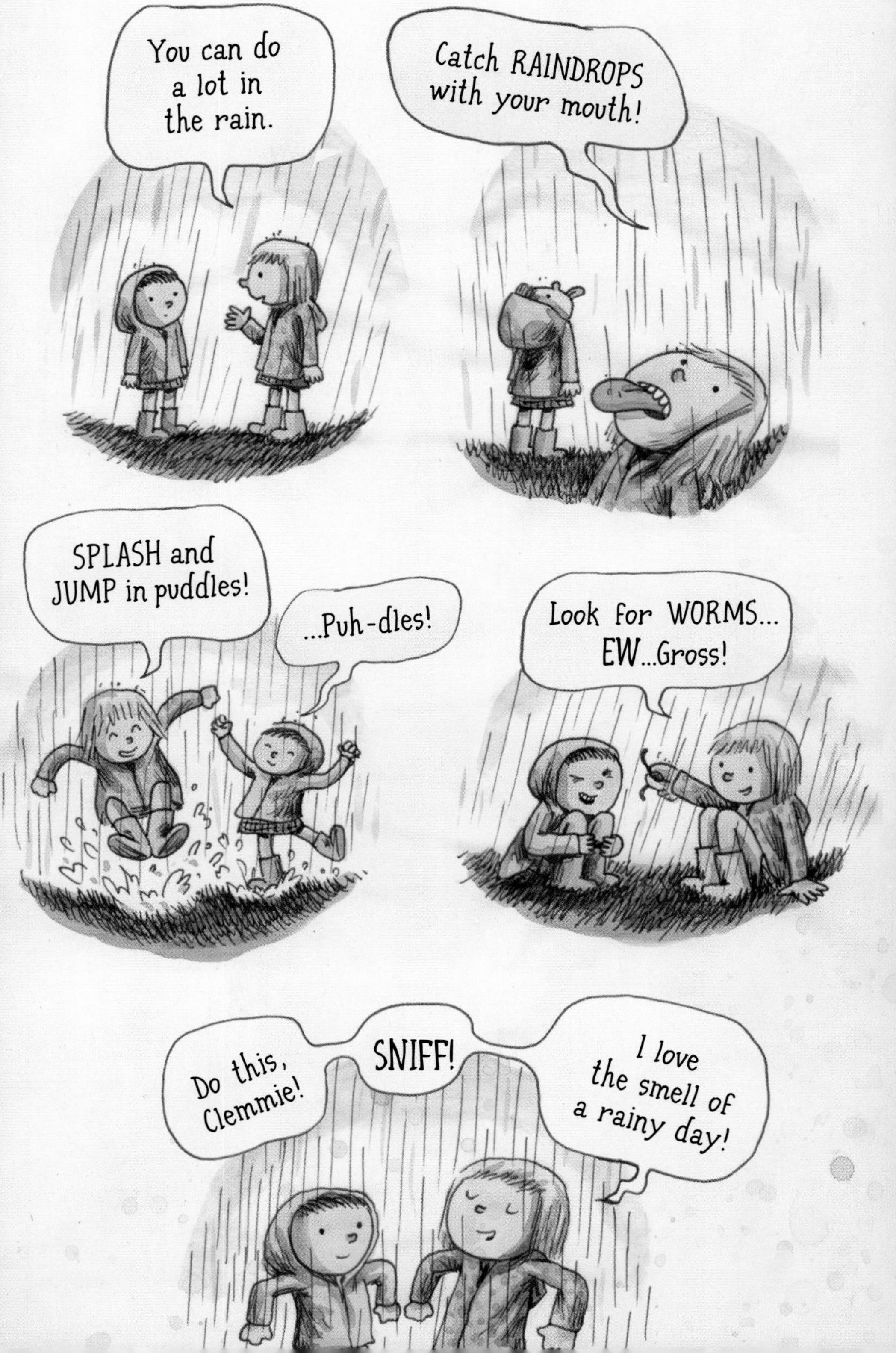
You can do a lot in the rain.
Catch RAINDROPS with your mouth!
SPLASH and JUMP in puddles!
...Puh-dles!
Look for WORMS... EW...Gross!
Do this, Clemmie!
SNIFF!
I love the smell of a rainy day!

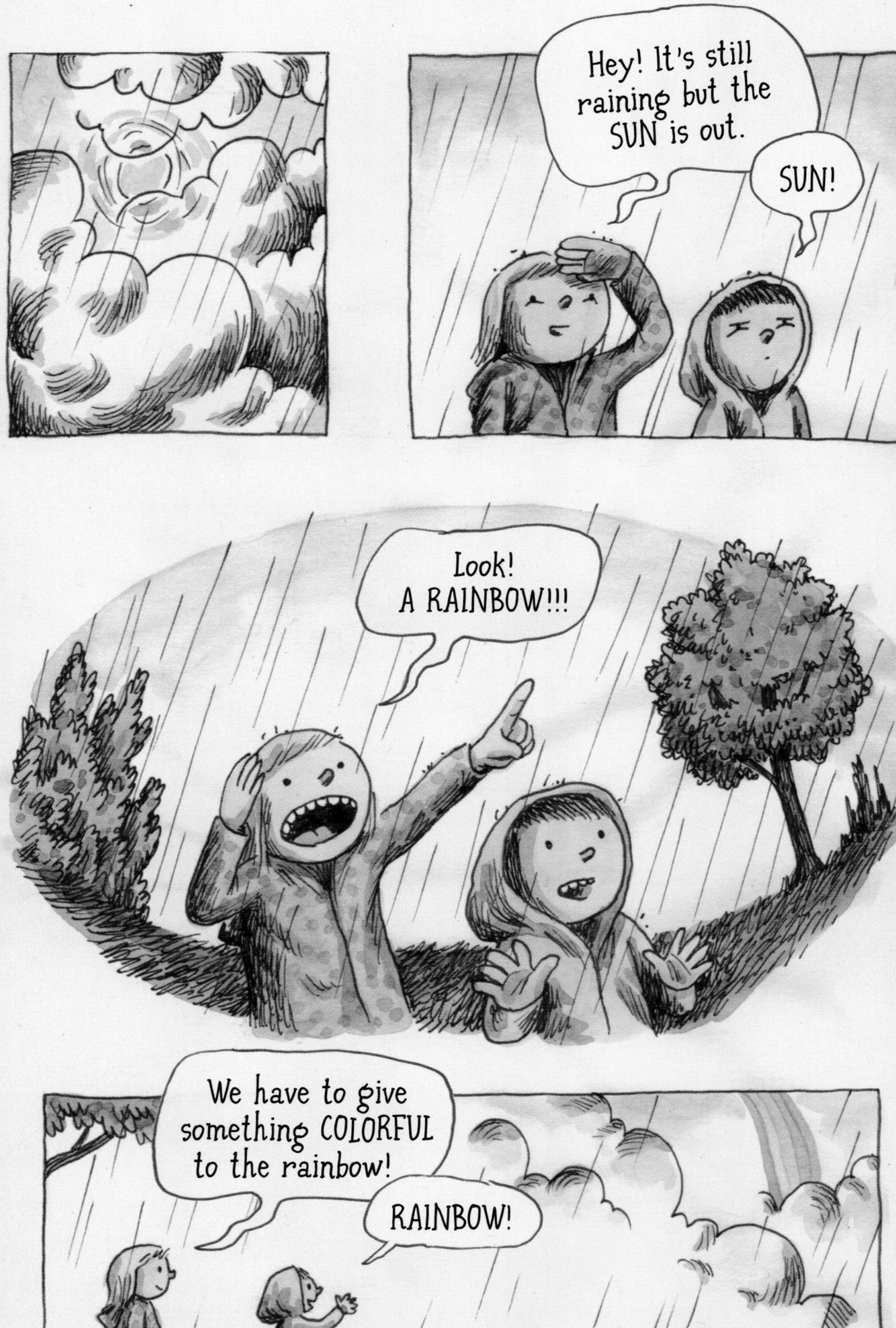
Hey! It's still raining but the SUN is out.
SUN!
Look! A RAINBOW!!!
We have to give something COLORFUL to the rainbow!
RAINBOW!

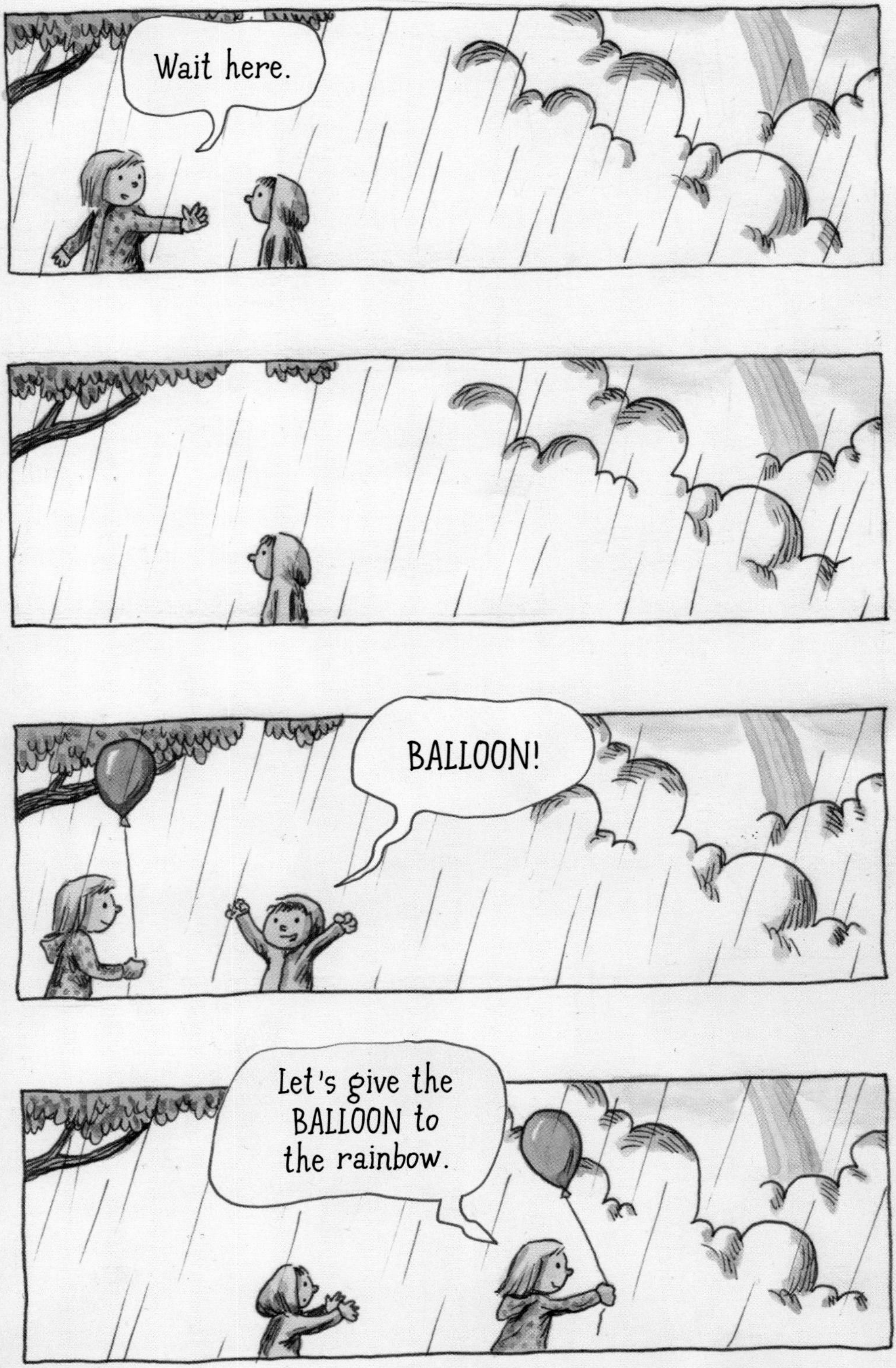
Wait here.
BALLOON!
Let's give the BALLOON to the rainbow.

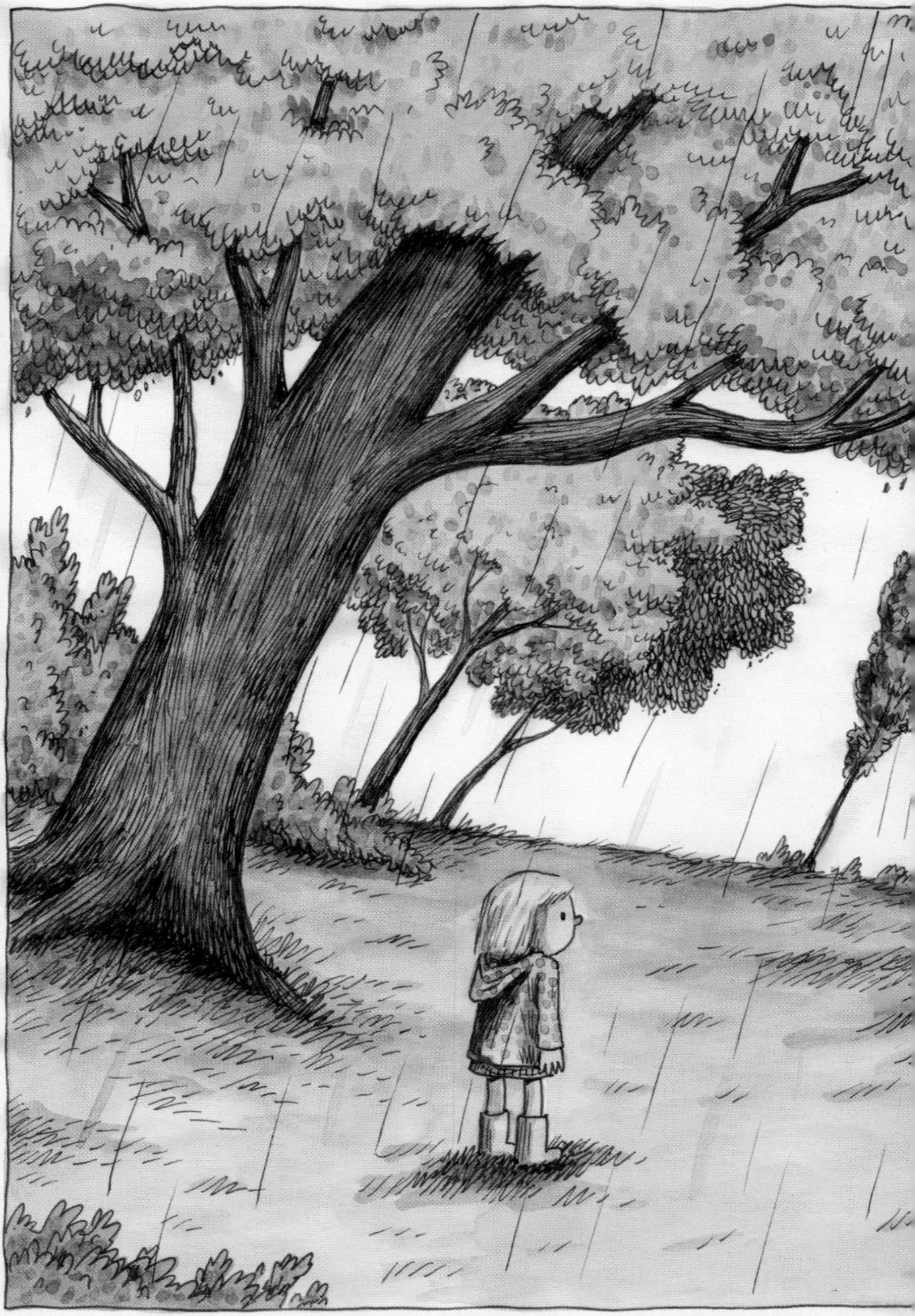

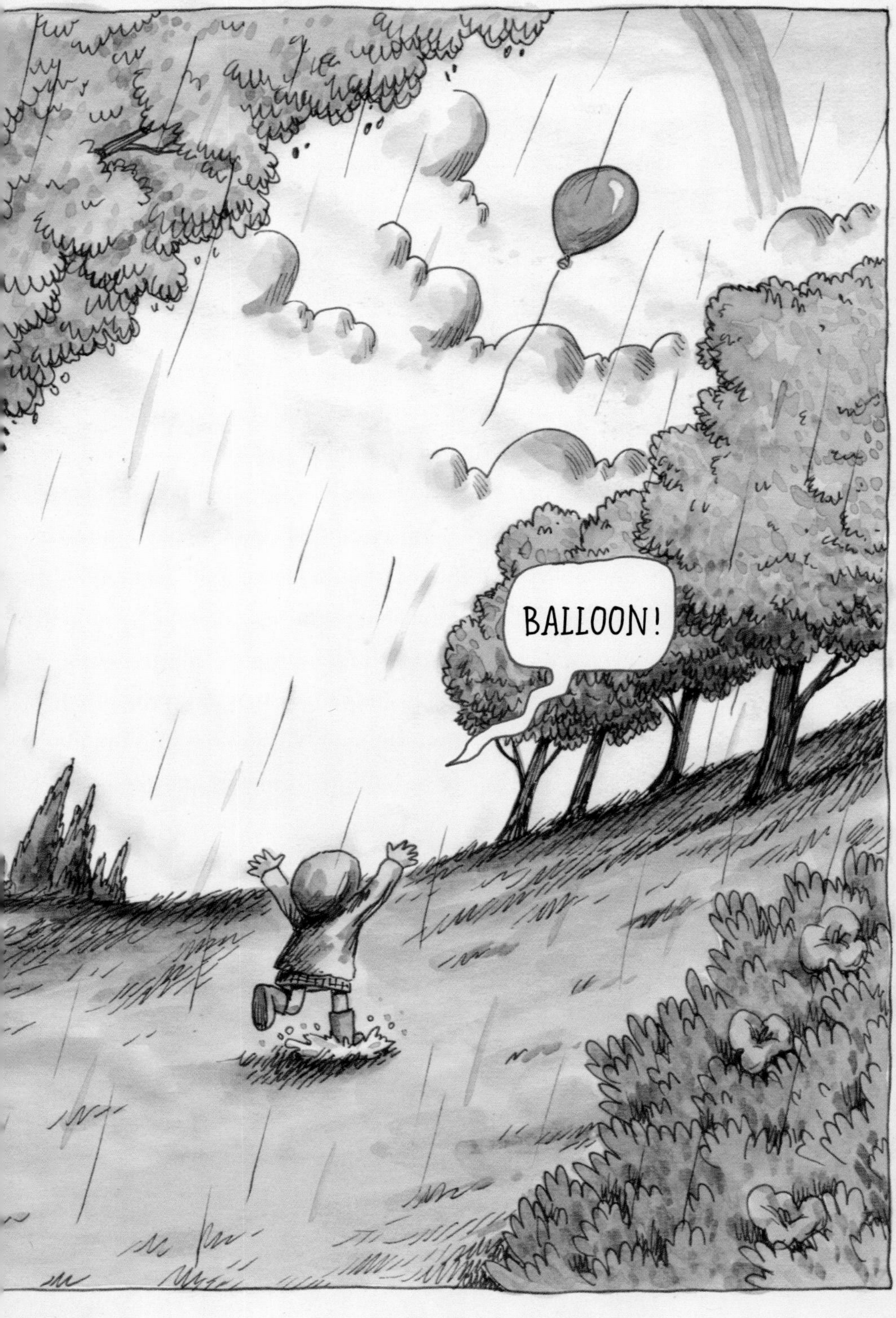
BALLOON!

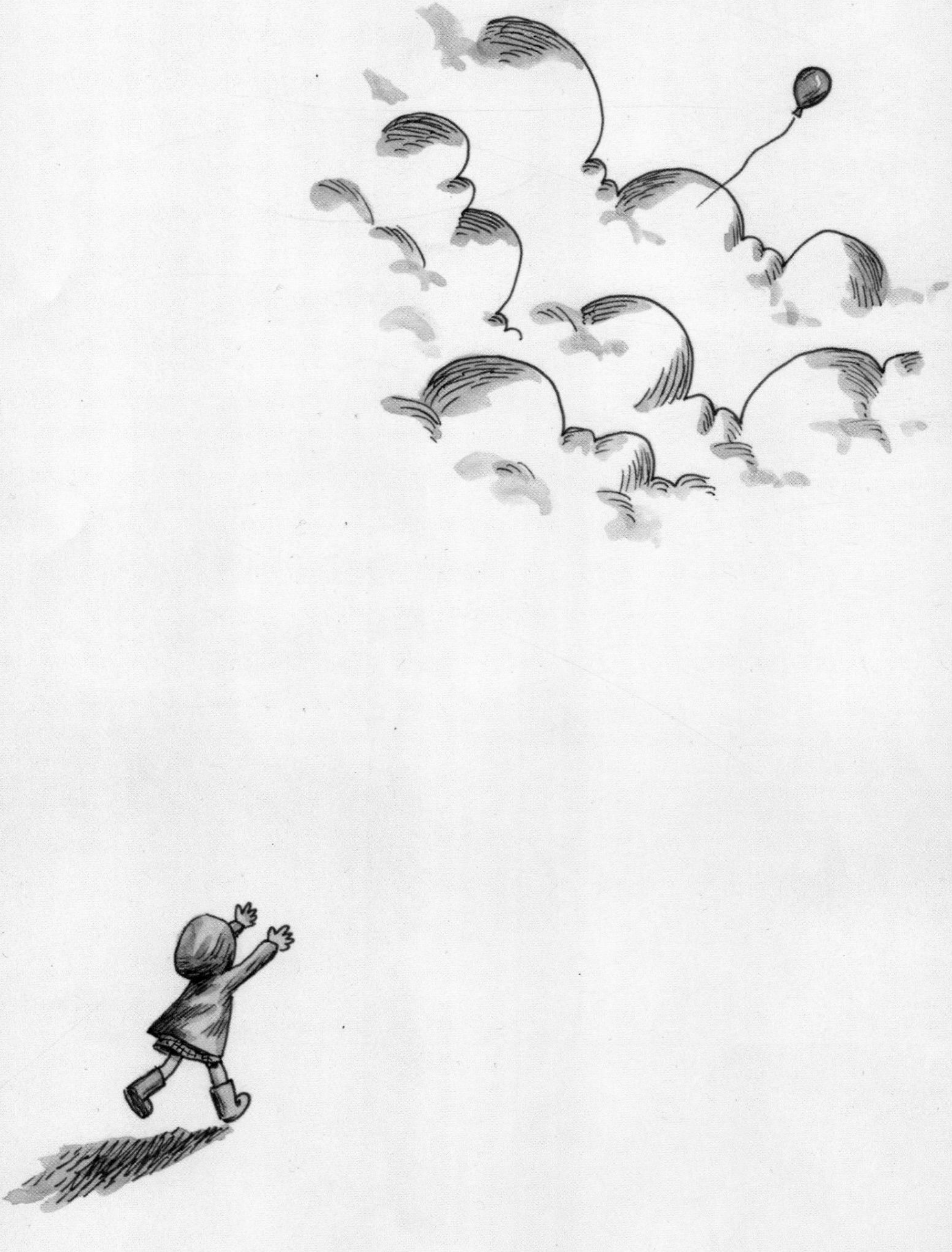

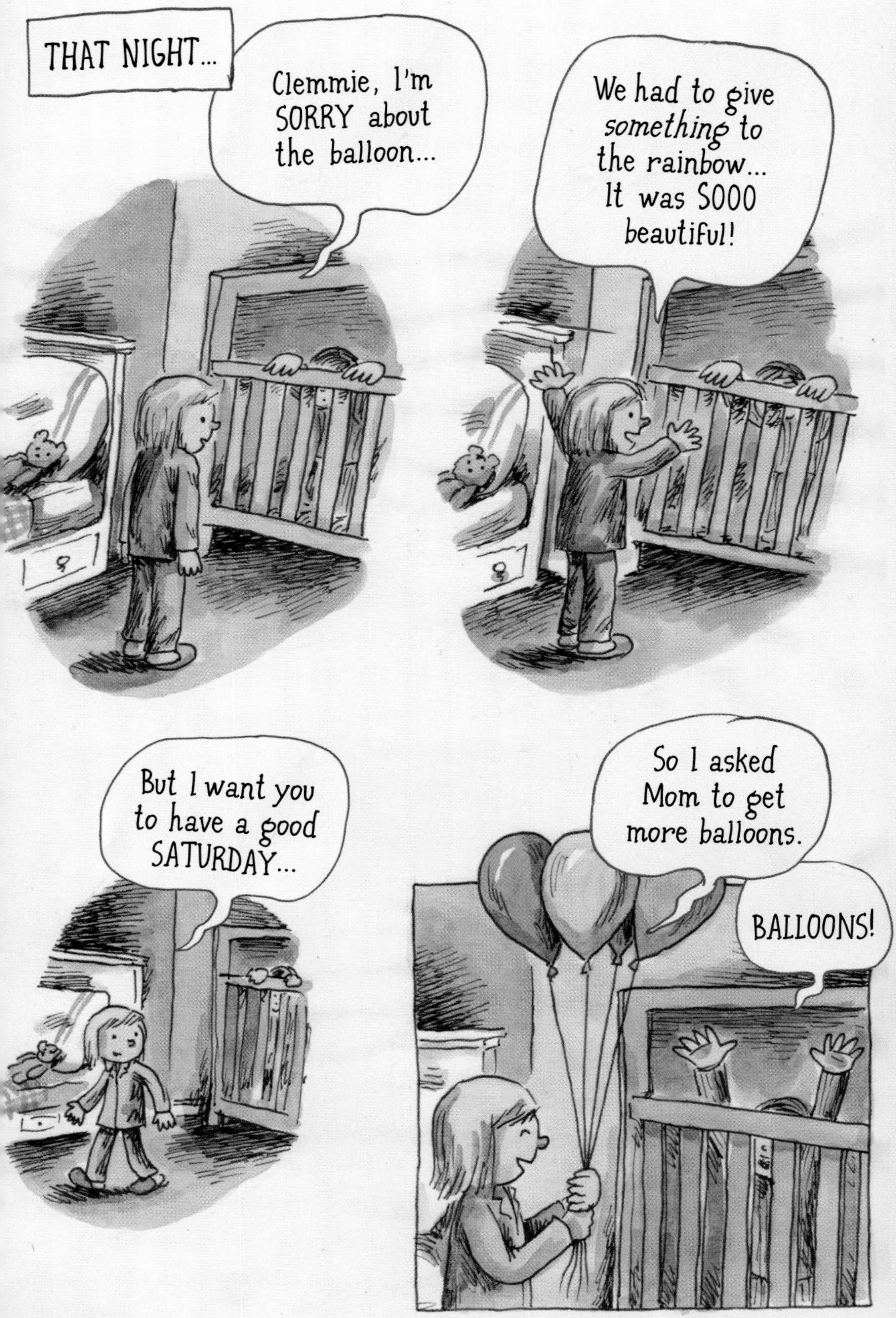
THAT NIGHT...
Clemmie, I'm SORRY about the balloon...
We had to give *something* to the rainbow... It was SOOO beautiful!
But I want you to have a good SATURDAY...
So I asked Mom to get more balloons.
BALLOONS!

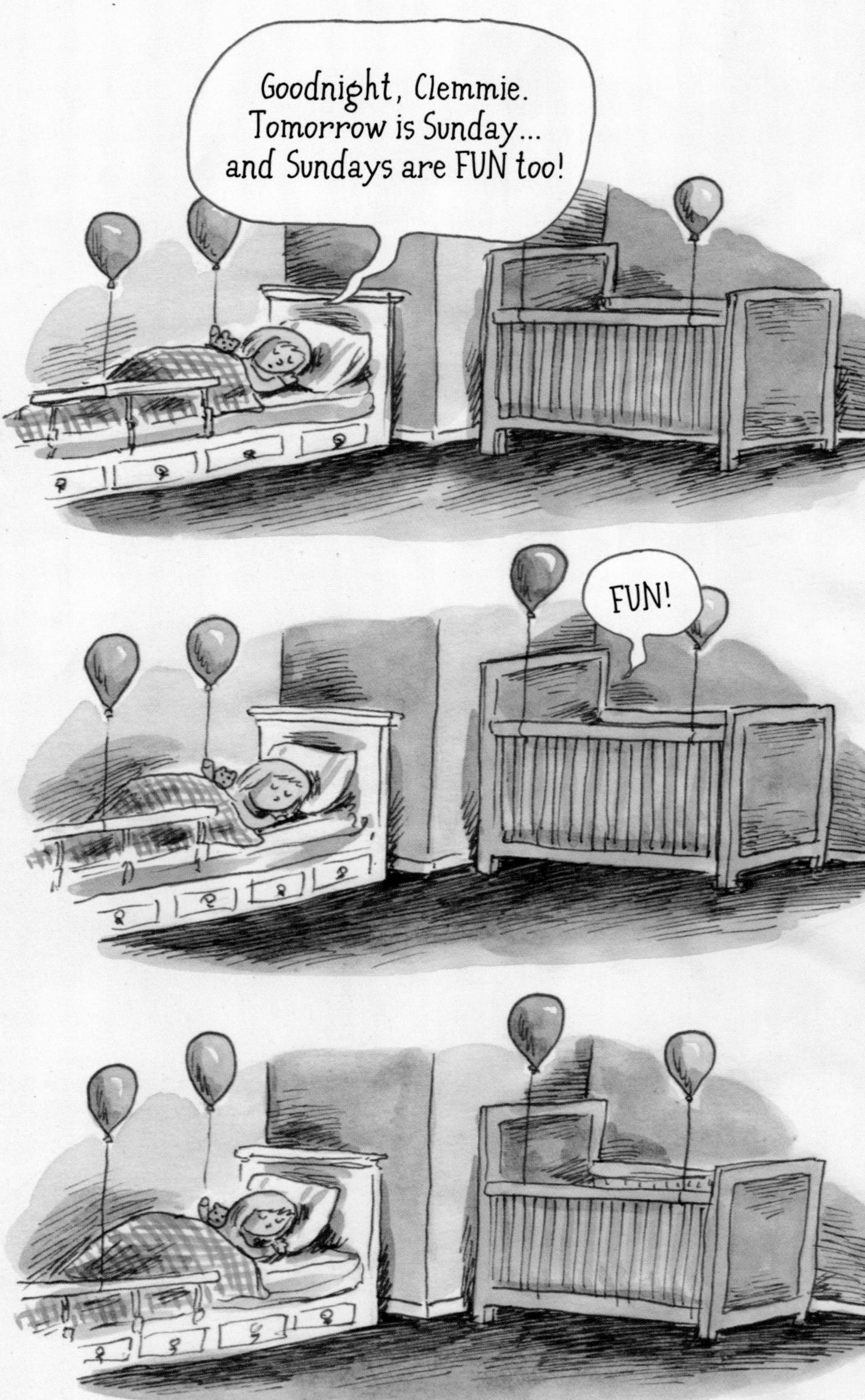
Goodnight, Clemmie.
Tomorrow is Sunday...
and Sundays are FUN too!
FUN!

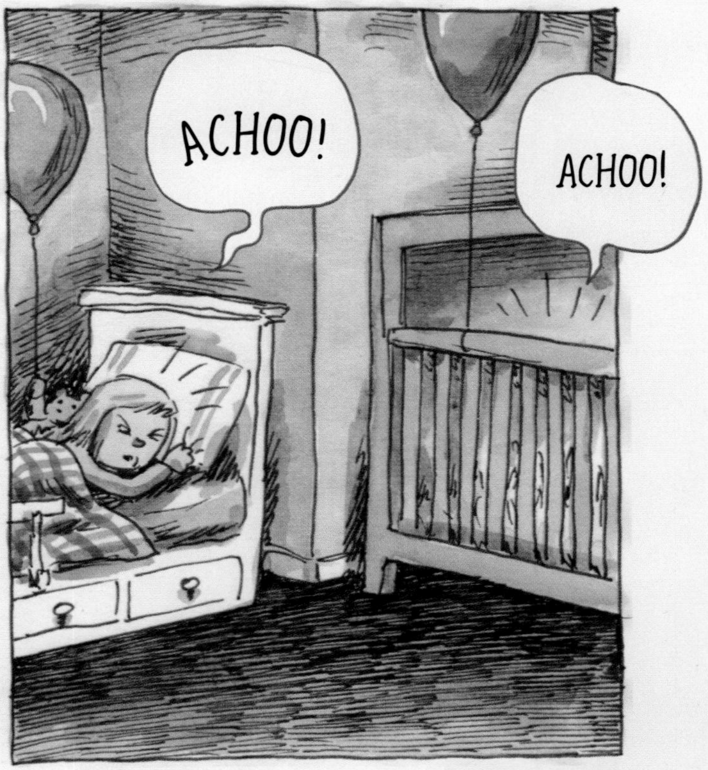
ACHOO!
ACHOO!

THE END

ABOUT THE AUTHOR

RICARDO LINIERS SIRI lives in Buenos Aires with his wife and two daughters, Matilda, 5, and Clementina, 3, who inspired this story. For more than ten years, he has published a hugely popular daily strip, *Macanudo*, in the Argentine newspaper *La Nación*. He also tours the world drawing on stage with musician Kevin Johansen. His work has been published in nine countries from Brazil to the Czech Republic, but this is his first book in the United States. Like his daughters, Liniers likes rainy days even more than sunny ones.

—by Matilda, 5

HOW TO READ COMICS WITH KIDS

Kids **love** comics! They are naturally drawn to the details in the pictures, which make them want to read the words. Comics beg for repeated readings and let both emerging and reluctant readers enjoy complex stories with a rich vocabulary. But since comics have their own grammar, here are a few tips for reading them with kids:

GUIDE YOUNG READERS: Use your finger to show your place in the text, but keep it at the bottom of the speaking character so it doesn't hide the very important facial expressions.

HAM IT UP! Think of the comic book story as a play and don't hesitate to read with expression and intonation. Assign parts or get kids to supply the sound effects, a great way to reinforce phonics skills.

LET THEM GUESS. Comics provide lots of context for the words, so emerging readers can make informed guesses. Like jigsaw puzzles, comics ask readers to make connections, so check a young audience's understanding by asking "What's this character thinking?" (but don't be surprised if a kid finds some of the comics' subtle details faster than you).

TALK ABOUT THE PICTURES. Point out how the artist paces the story with pauses (silent panels) or speeded-up action (a burst of short panels). Discuss how the size and shape of the panels carry meaning.

ABOVE ALL, ENJOY! There is of course never one right way to read, so go for the shared pleasure. Once children make the story happen in their imaginations, they have discovered the thrill of reading, and you won't be able to stop them. At that point, just go get them more books, and more comics.

www.TOON-BOOKS.com

SEE OUR FREE ONLINE CARTOON MAKERS, LESSON PLANS, AND MUCH MORE

TOON into Reading

LEVEL 1

GRADES K–1

LEXILE BR–100 • GUIDED READING A–J • READING RECOVERY 7–10

FIRST COMICS FOR BRAND-NEW READERS

- 200–300 easy sight words
- short sentences
- often one character
- single time frame or theme
- 1–2 panels per page

LEVEL 2

GRADES 1–2

LEXILE BR–170 • GUIDED READING G–M • READING RECOVERY 11–17

EASY-TO-READ COMICS FOR EMERGING READERS

- 300–600 words
- short sentences and repetition
- story arc with few characters in a small world
- 1–4 panels per page

LEVEL 3

GRADES 2–3

LEXILE 150–300 • GUIDED READING J–P • READING RECOVERY 17–19

CHAPTER-BOOK COMICS FOR ADVANCED BEGINNERS

- 800–1000+ words in long sentences
- long story divided in chapters
- broad world as well as shifts in time and place
- reader needs to make connections and speculate

COLLECT THEM ALL!

LEVEL 1 FIRST COMICS FOR BRAND-NEW READERS

A TRIP TO THE BOTTOM OF THE WORLD
With Mouse
Frank Viva

Little Mouse Gets Ready
THAT'S ME!
A TOON BOOK BY
Jeff Smith

CHICK & CHICKIE
PLAY ALL DAY!
What do you want to play?
I have a great idea...
A TOON BOOK BY
Claude Ponti

LEVEL 2 EASY-TO-READ COMICS FOR EMERGING READERS

BENNY AND PENNY
LIGHTS OUT!
Benny, where are you GOING?
A TOON BOOK BY
GEOFFREY HAYES

BENJAMIN BEAR
Bright Ideas!
A TOON BOOK BY
PHILIPPE COUDRAY

The big wet balloon
A TOON BOOK BY LINIERS

LUKE ON THE LOOSE
WHERE could those pigeons be hiding?
A TOON BOOK BY
HARRY BLISS

MAYA makes a MESS
RUTU MODAN

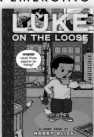

LEVEL 3 CHAPTER-BOOK COMICS FOR ADVANCED BEGINNERS

OTTO'S BACKWARDS DAY
A TOON BOOK BY
FRANK CAMMUSO
with JAY LYNCH

THE SHARK KING
R. KIKUO JOHNSON

ZIG AND WIKKI
THE COW
NADJA SPIEGELMAN & TRADE LOEFFLER

OTTO'S ORANGE DAY
I wish that EVERYTHING was orange!
A TOON BOOK BY
JAY LYNCH & FRANK CAMMUSO

MO AND JO
FIGHTING TOGETHER FOREVER
JAY LYNCH & DEAN HASPIEL

TOON BOOKS

Set 1 • 10 hardcover books	978-1-61479-147-8
Benny and Penny in Just Pretend	978-1-61479-148-5
Benny and Penny in the Toy Breaker	978-1-61479-149-2
Chick & Chickie Play All Day!	978-1-61479-150-8
Jack and the Box	978-1-61479-151-5
Mo and Jo Fighting Together Forever	978-1-61479-152-2
Nina in That Makes Me Mad!	978-1-61479-153-9
Otto's Orange Day	978-1-61479-154-6
Silly Lilly and the Four Seasons	978-1-61479-155-3
Silly Lilly in What Will I Be Today?	978-1-61479-156-0
Zig and Wikki in Something Ate My Homework	978-1-61479-157-7

Set 2 • 8 hardcover books	978-1-61479-298-7
Benjamin Bear in Fuzzy Thinking	978-1-61479-299-4
Benny and Penny in the Big No-No!	978-1-61479-300-7
Little Mouse Gets Ready	978-1-61479-301-4
Luke on the Loose	978-1-61479-302-1
Maya Makes a Mess	978-1-61479-303-8
Patrick in a Teddy Bear's Picnic and Other Stories	978-1-61479-304-5
The Shark King	978-1-61479-305-2
Zig and Wikki in the Cow	978-1-61479-306-9

Set 3 • 6 hardcover books	978-1-61479-422-6
Benjamin Bear in Bright Ideas!	978-1-61479-423-3
Benny and Penny in Lights Out!	978-1-61479-424-0
The Big Wet Balloon	978-1-61479-425-7
Otto's Backwards Day	978-1-61479-426-4
Patrick Eats His Peas and Other Stories	978-1-61479-427-1
A Trip to the Bottom of the World with Mouse	978-1-61479-428-8